Disney's Lilo & Stitch

Ladybird

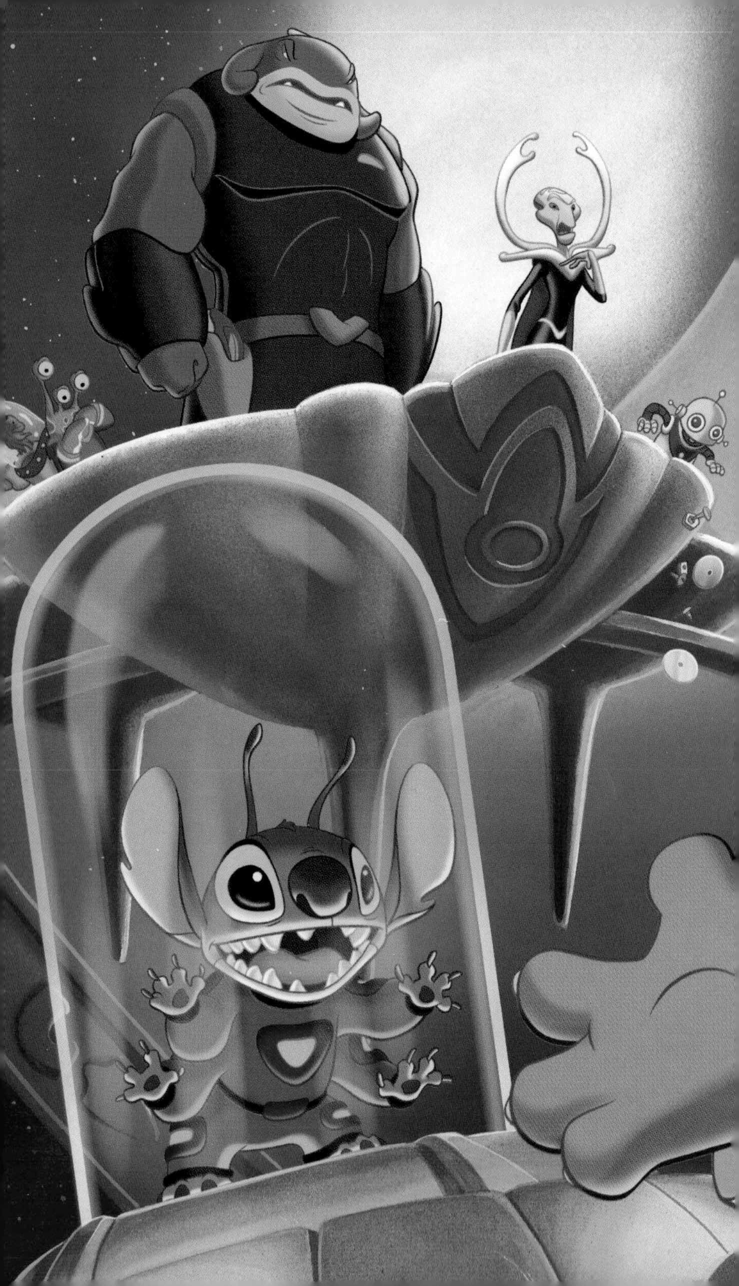

It all began on Planet Turo. The Galactic Federation had accused a scientist, Jumba Jukiba, of creating an illegal lifeform. Jumba was proud of Experiment 626. It had been designed to destroy things and was very wicked and evil indeed.

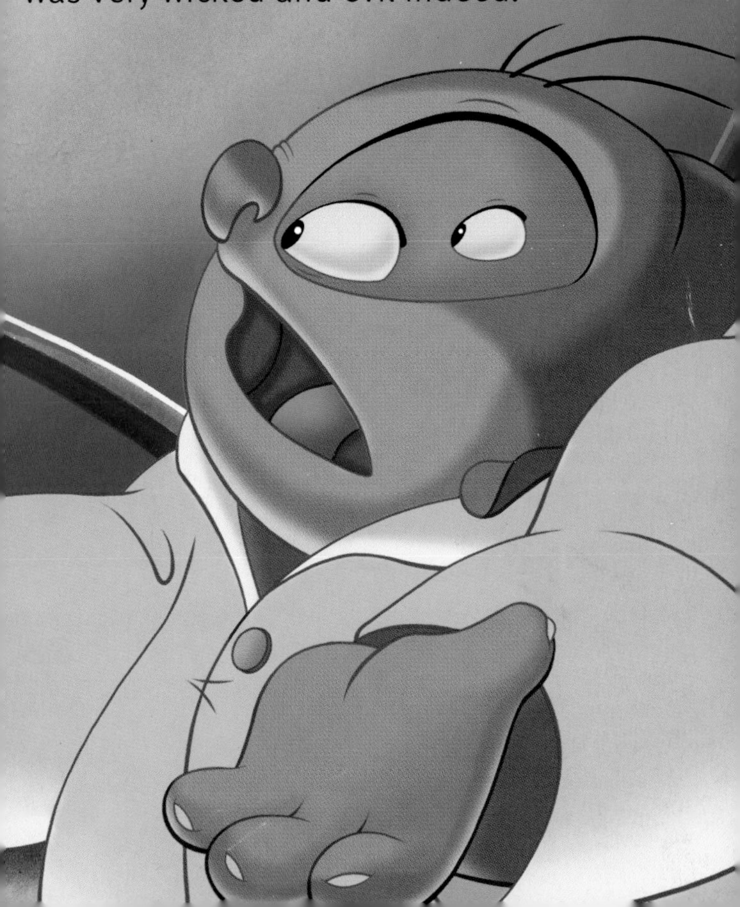

The Galactic Federation was shocked. "It must be destroyed!" said Captain Gantu. "Take him away," ordered the Grand Councilwoman.

Jumba was sent to prison, but the unstoppable Experiment 626 managed to escape! He stole a red police cruiser and zoomed off to freedom. The aliens tracked him as he headed towards Planet Earth.

The Grand Councilwoman turned to Pleakley, a nerdy alien and an expert on Planet Earth. He showed her his ViewMaster, so she could take a look at this far-off planet where Experiment 626 was headed.

The Grand Councilwoman had no choice. She released Jumba to capture Experiment 626 and sent Pleakley to keep an eye on Jumba.

Meanwhile, on a beautiful Hawaiian island on Earth, a little girl called Lilo swam out to feed her favourite fish before heading off to hula school.

Lilo was quite naughty during class and afterwards none of the other girls would play with her, so she wandered off alone. Later, when Nani, Lilo's older sister, arrived to pick her up and couldn't find her, she panicked!

Today was a big day. The social worker was coming and could take Lilo into foster care. "You'd better be at home, Lilo," Nani said to herself, running as fast as she could.

Nani had looked after Lilo since their parents died . . . and taking care of Lilo wasn't easy.

Nani found Lilo at home, listening to records and sulking. When the social worker, Cobra Bubbles, arrived he looked around the untidy house and at the pans bubbling over on the cooker. He realised that Lilo had been at home alone.

“This visit did not go well,” he told Nani. “You have three days to change my mind.”

Nani was cross with Lilo for not waiting at hula school and they quarrelled.

That night, Nani heard her sister wishing for a friend of her own. Maybe a pet would help, thought Nani.

Meanwhile, where was Experiment 626? Soon after crash landing on Earth, he was hit by a truck. Being indestructible, he survived and was taken to an animal rescue centre. Jumba and Pleakley, who had followed Stitch to Earth, hung around outside, watching and waiting.

And there Lilo found him. He gave her a big hug – she could be his ticket out of here – and Lilo fell in love with him. "His name is Stitch," she said. Nani wasn't happy, but she gave in.

As they left, Jumba took aim with a plasma cannon. Nasty Stitch used Lilo as a shield!

Nani went to work, leaving Lilo with Stitch. Stitch scampered all over the island, looking for something to wreck. Lilo tagged along, with Jumba and Pleakley never far behind.

Later, Lilo and Stitch went to the hotel where Nani worked. Stitch ate a lot and had terrible table manners. They watched a firedancer called David. He wanted to date Nani, but she was always too busy.

Pleakley and Jumba were there, too, in disguise. They made a grab for Stitch, and Stitch tried to swallow Pleakley's head! There was a bit of a commotion, and Nani's boss came over. He fired her.

Lilo, Stitch and Nani trudged home.
"We have to take Stitch back to the animal rescue centre, Lilo. He's creepy, and I don't even think he's a dog," said Nani as patiently as she could.

"But he was an orphan and we adopted him!" cried Lilo. "What about '*ohana*? Dad said '*ohana* means family, and family means nobody gets left behind, or forgotten." Nani gave in.

That night, Stitch found a photo of Lilo's lost family. She snatched it back. "Don't touch that!" she cried. Stitch went crazy. He broke things, he tore things up, he destroyed everything he could until, at last, Lilo managed to calm him down.

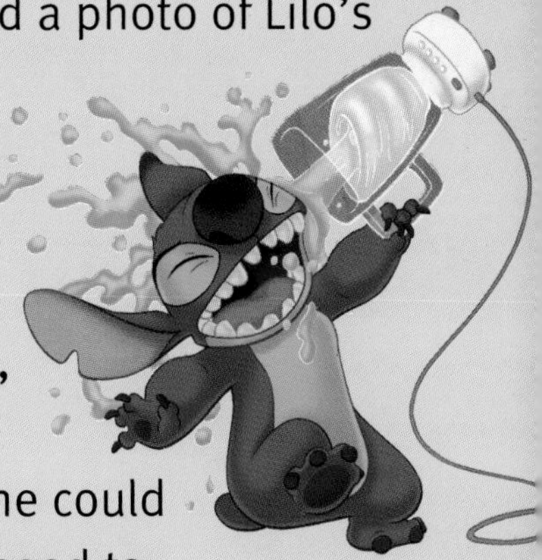

A few days later, Cobra paid another visit. He warned Nani she must find another job

She looked hard, but Stitch always ruined her chances. He caused havoc in the supermarket, the cafe, in the smart hotel and even on the beach when Nani applied to be a lifeguard.

Lilo and Nani felt glum, but they cheered up when David offered to take them surfing!

Down at the general store, Nani was offered the job! She was so happy, she rushed back to tell Lilo.

At home she couldn't believe her eyes. The house was on fire and Cobra had Lilo. "Please don't take her," Nani pleaded. "I have no choice," said Cobra sadly. While he and Nani argued, Lilo ran away.

Stitch followed Lilo and showed her that he was an alien, and not a dog at all. She was shocked, and angry that he had lied. Suddenly, Captain Gantu captured them. Stitch escaped, but Lilo was trapped!

On Planet Turo, the Grand Councilwoman was getting impatient. She contacted Jumba and Pleakley, fired them, and put Captain Gantu on the job. This made Jumba even more determined to find Stitch. And now he could do it his way!

Later, Lilo and Nani were at home when David knocked at the door. He'd found Nani a job, but she had to hurry. Before she ran out of the house, she turned to Lilo. "Stay here for a few minutes," she said. "I'll be right back. Lock the door."

A little later, Stitch burst through the dog door, followed by Jumba firing his plasma cannon. Pleakley appeared soon after. Stitch and Jumba fought wildly in the house, smashing everything in their way. The house was a mess.

Eventually Lilo rang Cobra for help.

Jumba and Pleakley were nearby. “Come on,” said Jumba. “We’re going swimming!”

Stitch loved surfing, until Jumba tried to pull him under. Stitch grabbed onto Lilo, almost drowning her. Luckily, Nani and David came to the rescue.

Cobra was watching and had seen Lilo nearly drown. He was sure to take her into care now. Stitch was suddenly sad. He realised it was all his fault.

Nani caught up with Stitch, and watched Captain Gantu's ship soar into the sky with Lilo trapped inside. Nani whacked Stitch with a branch. "Where's Lilo?" she demanded. "I know you had something to do with this." He turned round, and BOOM! Jumba blasted him with his plasma gun and Pleakley arrested him.

After Pleakley reported in to the Grand Councilwoman, Stitch looked at Jumba. "Help us find Lilo!" he pleaded in their own language. And, to his own surprise, and Pleakley's, Jumba agreed to help.

They all – including Nani – climbed into Jumba and Pleakley's big red spacecraft and chased after Lilo. Gantu fired at them, but the red ship followed until eventually, they rescued Lilo! Jumba crash-landed into the sea, but David was surfing nearby and gave them a ride to the shore.

Lilo, Nani and David were very surprised to see aliens on the beach, including the Grand Councilwoman. "Take Experiment 626 to my ship," she said.

"Leave him alone!" pleaded Lilo.

"This is my family," said Stitch. "I found it all on my own. It's little, and broken, but it's still good."

"I paid two dollars for him. I own him," Lilo cried. "If you take him, you're stealing!"

The Grand Councilwoman believed strongly in rules. She decided to let him stay. The aliens went home, leaving Jumba and Pleakley behind. They, along with Cobra and David, helped to rebuild Lilo and Nani's home.

Lilo was happy. She had a family again.